WHEN
PARROTS SPEAK

LINDA BOZZO

Enslow Publishing
101 W. 23rd Street
Suite 240
New York, NY 10011
USA

enslow.com

WORDS TO KNOW

captivity Held or confined to keep from escaping.

communicate To pass information from one to another.

fossil A trace, a print, or the remains of a plant or animal from a past age.

mimicking Copying without understanding.

predators Animals that hunt other animals for food.

social animals Animals who enjoy friendly relationships with others.

species A group of animals that can breed among themselves.

vocal learning The ability to make new sounds by mimicking.

CONTENTS

Words to Know **2**

Chapter One . . . .
Amazing Alex **4**

Chapter Two
Bird Brains **11**

Chapter Three
Look Who's Talking **18**

Chapter Four
Feathered Friends **24**

Learn More **31**
Index **32**

AMAZING ALEX

In June of 1977, researcher Dr. Irene Pepperberg walked into a Chicago pet store. She asked the person who worked with the birds to choose a parrot for her. At the time Alex, an African gray parrot, was around a year old. But Alex wouldn't be an ordinary pet. He was about to become the subject of many studies. Dr. Pepperberg hoped Alex would help her better understand how parrots could not only learn speech from humans but could also **communicate** with them.

Dr. Pepperberg created experiments. She applied for grants. It took many hours and lots of money to study Alex. Dr. Pepperberg worked with Alex eight to twelve hours a day. She played games with him,

African grays, like Alex, are known to be among the best talkers in the parrot family. Alex and Dr. Pepperberg worked together for thirty years at Brandeis University.

As Dr. Pepperberg's research went on, she realized that Alex wasn't just reciting words. Through hours of playing games together, Alex was learning and thinking for himself.

offering rewards for correct answers. Alex loved being the center of attention. But things didn't always go smoothly. Some days, Alex was in a bad mood and wasn't easy to work with. He would give her all the wrong answers, cleverly avoiding the correct ones. This showed that Alex really did know the answers. Other days he worked very well.

Dr. Pepperberg asked Alex simple questions such as, "What color?" when holding up an object. Alex would reply with a simple answer such as, "Orange." When Alex was correct, Dr. Pepperberg rewarded him with praise. "Good parrot," she would say. She also rewarded Alex with delicious treats of fruits and vegetables when he labeled them correctly. Dr. Pepperberg worked with Alex on number tasks and shape questions. She even taught Alex what type of matter certain objects were made of.

Dr. Pepperberg did study after study to test how smart Alex was. She worked long hours gathering research to prove that Alex understood what she was saying. One day Dr. Pepperberg asked Alex, "What color is corn?" Even though there was no corn that Alex could see, he answered, "Yellow." He could look at two objects and tell her what was the same or different about them, like color or shape. He could tell her which object was bigger and which was smaller. Talk about smart!

While learning colors, Alex looked at himself in the mirror and asked, "What color?" This was a clue that Alex wasn't **mimicking** Dr. Pepperberg. This showed that Alex was learning. He was able to think about himself as a living thing. Dr. Pepperberg kept creating more advanced tasks for Alex.

Each night Alex told Dr. Pepperberg, "You be good. Bye." Dr. Pepperberg would answer with,

Not a Birdbrain

By the time he was thirty-one, Alex knew more than one hundred words and the names of fifty objects and their colors. He could ask and answer simple questions. He could even count to eight and do simple math, as well as many other amazing tasks.

Alex and Dr. Pepperberg shared an extraordinary bond. It was through their relationship that Dr. Pepperberg was able to uncover cognitive abilities in Alex that no one believed were possible.

"Bye." Alex would then say, "I love you." Dr. Pepperberg would reply by saying, "I love you, too. I'll see you tomorrow."

Sadly, on the night of September 6, 2007, Alex passed away suddenly. He was only thirty-one years old. This is young for an African gray parrot. A deep loss was felt when Alex died. He was one of the most famous birds in the world.

CHAPTER TWO

BIRD BRAINS

No one knows exactly when parrots first appeared on Earth. **Fossils** tell us that parrot-type birds lived some forty million years ago. What we do know is that parrots have a long history of being popular pets. Ancient Egyptians are thought to have been the first to keep African gray parrots as pets.

What makes parrots so popular? They live long lives—often more than fifty years. Parrots are certainly some of the most beautiful birds on this planet. They are colorful and playful. Parrots are probably most famous for being able to mimic sounds and learn human speech. This means they can speak to us in our own language. Many people enjoy the company these talking birds provide.

Ancient Egyptians kept animals as pets. Their pets were so important to them that they honored them in paintings and on the walls of their tombs.

Parrots have small heads, which means their brains are quite small. So what makes these birds so smart? This question has been puzzling scientists for a long time. Don't judge a brain by its size! New studies show it may be what's inside the brain that matters. Researchers have been trying to figure out why some types of birds are better at mimicking than others. What they found is that parrots have more brain cells packed in their tiny skulls than some large mammals, like apes and monkeys. Researchers think that the tightly-packed brain cells may help birds to learn more quickly.

In one study scientists used a special device to count brain cells in thirty-two different bird **species**, including parrots. The researchers found that birds scored big in the brain cell department. Other than the difference in the number of brain cells, scientists have found differences in the structure of parrots' brains. This may help explain why parrots can learn speech and sounds as well as they do. But there's more!

Macaws are the largest parrots in the world. Scarlet macaws, like the one pictured here, can measure as long as 33 inches (84 centimeters) from their beak to their tail feathers.

A new study has found that parrots have "cores" in their brains that control **vocal learning**. What makes them different from other vocal birds, such as songbirds and hummingbirds? The answer is that parrots also have "shells" or outer rings in their brains. These outer rings are also used in vocal learning. This shell region might explain why parrots can imitate better than other vocal learning species. However, more studies need to be done to prove that this is true.

Scientists continue to research parrots and how they are able to learn sounds and develop speech. They hope to unlock more secrets about these amazing birds, their brains, and how they speak.

Scarlet macaws are known to be very intelligent. They can perform tricks and learn to speak. They are also very affectionate birds filled with personality, making them popular pets.

The Syrinx

Parrots don't have vocal chords to produce sound like humans. Instead, they have a special vocal organ known as a syrinx. The air from the parrot's lungs passes through the syrinx and produces sounds.

Since parrots are the only birds that use their tongues like humans do to be vocal, scientists may also better understand human speech by studying parrots. That's great news for both species!

CHAPTER THREE

LOOK WHO'S TALKING

From small songbirds to large macaws, parrots are **social animals**. They enjoy being a part of those around them. When kept as pets, parrots will want to be with their owners. They will want to feel part of the family. But be careful what you say. A parrot will often repeat what it hears. Some parrots will only squawk or repeat sounds such as the telephone ringing or the microwave beeping. Other parrots might say words such as "hello" or "pretty bird."

How do parrots learn to speak? Parrots are vocal-learning birds. This means they are able to learn to make new sounds. They are not born with this ability. Vocal learners must hear the sounds they are trying to mimic. Scientists believe there is something special about the brains of these animals that let them mimic sounds and learn to speak.

There are only a few types of birds that can learn human speech. They include mynah birds, ravens, and of course parrots, who tend to be best at it.

Birds can make wonderful companions. Teaching parrots to talk, whistle, or do tricks makes them delightful pets.

But parrots are just one of three of the main groups of vocal-learning birds. The others are songbirds and hummingbirds. Scientists believe that songbirds, such as the cardinal, learn to sing the way human babies learn to speak. Young songbirds begin by listening and memorizing what they hear from adult birds. They then mimic and practice the sounds. Songbirds take bits of sound. By putting sounds together they make songs. A few kinds of songbirds, like canaries, can learn new songs their entire lives. Others are not able to learn new songs

The Truth About Cats and Dogs

Dogs bark. Cats meow. It's not learned. They are able to do this from birth. Scientists say that animals like these aren't able to learn to bark or meow in a new way. This is because, unlike parrots, they are not vocal learners.

Like parrots, hummingbirds are vocal learners. They also can beat their wings very rapidly. In flight, they make a loud trilling noise with their wing tips.

Parrots learn human speech while they are safe in captivity. Being able to mimic this speech wouldn't help them in the wild!

after they reach a certain age. They are called closed-ended vocal learners.

Hummingbirds are believed to also be vocal learners. But you have to listen carefully as they zip from flower to flower. Their chirping sounds come from their voice box and are not very loud. The humming sound that gives the hummingbird its name, comes not from its vocals but from the fast beating of its wings!

Wild birds will mimic the sounds they learn in the wild. Perhaps these sounds help keep them safe from **predators**. But birds that learn human speech must do so in **captivity**. Safe in good homes, pet parrots learn to speak for fun and to feel like part of the family. Pet parrots that have escaped from households have been known to pass phrases from their owners onto birds in the wild. You can only hope they're phrases that are worth repeating!

CHAPTER FOUR

FEATHERED FRIENDS

At the beginning of its training, a talking parrot will start making noises. Over time, these sounds will turn into words. This is also how human children begin to speak. Learning anything new takes time. It's important to know the more language parrots hear, the more language they will learn.

When teaching a parrot to speak it's important to repeat words and phrases over and over again. Your bird will want to copy your voice. If your bird repeats something you don't want her to repeat, don't let it ruffle your feathers. Instead, just ignore her.

Fact

Parakeets are a type of parrot. Male parakeets are more likely to talk than females.

A pet parrot won't only learn to mimic human speech. It might also begin to bark like the family dog.

Treats are an excellent way to encourage your bird to respond to commands. Find a special reward that your bird loves most and use it only during training sessions.

When your feathered friend doesn't get the attention she seeks, she will stop saying it. Parrots will also repeat sounds. So don't be surprised if your parrot meows like your cat or barks like your dog.

Pet birds tend to learn words that are related to things they want. Take food, for example. You can start by teaching your parrot the names of the foods. It will help if you give the bird the food item as a reward when it starts making a sound that is close to the word.

Common words parrots learn rather quickly are "hello" and "goodbye." For one, they are simple words. They are also words often spoken in a household. If you are excited about saying a word, chances are your parrot will be too! Most pet parrots are simply mimicking you, unlike the parrots researchers professionally train to understand human language.

Your bird might not repeat your words right away. He will likely speak when he wants your attention. But not all birds that can speak, will speak.

Parrots will let it be known when they don't like each other. They will squawk, peck, or even chase each other.

Hablas Español?

A British parrot named Nigel went missing. When he returned to his owner four years later he no longer had his British accent, and he spoke only in Spanish!

If a bird is frightened it might not speak. If there is more than one bird in the household it may already be getting enough attention from its companion.

If a young bird can mimic sounds, chances are you can teach it to speak words. If you want to be sure your parrot will speak, adopt an older bird who already knows how. Keep in mind that talking parrots can be loud! And while a parrot can be a wonderful member of your family, they need lots of time and hard work.

There is still much we don't know about parrots. New tools and experiments are being used all the time to study birds. Brain scans help scientists see a live bird's brain at work. This gives them a closer look into what is going on in a bird's mind. Experiments, like those being done by Dr. Pepperberg, are helpful, too. Because parrots are so smart, studying them could teach us about the minds of other species. Studying the way parrots speak could hold a bright future for learning more about human speech. One thing we know for sure: when parrots speak, we should listen!

LEARN MORE

Books

Bjorklund, Ruth. *Parrots*. New York, NY: Children's Press. 2013.

Howard, Fran. *Parrots*. North Mankato, MN.: Capstone Press. 2013.

Owen, Ruth. *Parrots*. New York, NY: Windmill Books. 2012.

Roth, Susan L., and Cindy Trumbore. *Parrots Over Puerto Rico*. New York, NY: Lee & Low Books. 2013.

DVD

Wick, Emily, Arlene Levin Rowe, and Irene M. Pepperberg. *Life with Alex: A Memoir*. Grey Parrot Studios. 2012.

Websites

The Alex Foundation

http://alexfoundation.org/the-birds/alex/

Learn more about and view photos of Alex the famous African gray parrot!

NOVA

http://www.pbs.org/wgbh/nova/nature/profile-irene-pepperberg-alex.html

Watch a video of Dr. Pepperberg working with her amazing African gray parrot Alex.

San Diego Zoo

http://animals.sandiegozoo.org/animals/parrot

Fun facts about parrots and how they live in the wild.

INDEX

A
African gray parrots, 4, 10, 11, 15
Alex (African gray parrot), 4–10
B
brain cells, 13
brains, 13–15
C
communication, 4
E
Egypt, ancient, 11
F
fossils, 11

H
hummingbirds, 15, 20, 23
I
intelligence, 13
L
learning, 7–8
M
mimicry, 8, 11, 13, 18–19, 20, 23, 27, 29
N
Nigel (parrot), 29
O
ornithology, 20

P
Pepperberg, Irene, 4–10, 30
pets, history of, 11
S
social behaviors, 18
songbirds, 15, 18, 20
syrinx, 17
T
teaching, 24–29
tongues, 17
V
vocal learning, 15, 18, 20–23

Published in 2018 by Enslow Publishing, LLC.
101 W. 23rd Street, Suite 240, New York, NY 10011

Library of Congress Cataloging-in-Publication Data

Names: Bozzo, Linda.
Title: When parrots speak / Linda Bozzo.
Description: New York : Enslow Publishing, 2018. | Series: Animal emotions | Includes bibliographical references and index. | Audience: Grades 3 to 5.
Identifiers: LCCN 2017003416| ISBN 9780766086210 (library-bound) | ISBN 9780766088641 (pbk.) | ISBN 9780766088580 (6-pack)
Subjects: LCSH: Parrots–Psychology–Juvenile literature. | Parrots–Behavior–Juvenile literature. | Human-animal communication–Juvenile literature.
Classification: LCC SF473.P3 B65 2017 | DDC 636.6/865–dc23
LC record available at https://lccn.loc.gov/2017003416

Printed in the United States of America

To Our Readers: We have done our best to make sure all website addresses in this book were active and appropriate when we went to press. However, the author and the publisher have no control over and assume no liability for the material available on those websites or on any websites they may link to. Any comments or suggestions can be sent by e-mail to customerservice@enslow.com.

Photo Credits: Cover, p. 1 Mint Images - Frans Lanting/Getty Images; pp. 4, 5, 11, 18, 24 Rick Friedman/Corbis Historical/Getty Images; p. 6 Michael Goldman/The LIFE Images Collection/Getty Images; p. 9 Anacleto Rapping/Los Angeles Times/Getty Images; p. 12 Radius Images/Getty Images; p. 14 Dirk Freder/E+/Getty Images; p. 16 Mark Johnson/NIS/Minden Pictures/Getty Images; p. 19 Lane Oatey/Blue Jean Images/Getty Images; p. 21 Russell Burden/Photolibrary/Getty Images; p. 22 Philomena Bradt/EyeEm/Getty Images; p. 25 Barcroft Media/Getty Images; p. 26 Viktoria Rodriguez/EyeEm/Getty Images; p. 28 Ted Horowitz/Corbis/Getty Images; interior pages background image De Space Studio/Shutterstock.com.